Margery Cuyler

From Here to There

illustrated by Yu Cha Pak

Henry Holt and Company
New York

Henry Holt and Company, Inc., *Publishers since 1866*
115 West 18th Street, New York, New York 10011

Henry Holt is a registered trademark of Henry Holt and Company, Inc.

Library of Congress Cataloging-in-Publication Data
Cuyler, Margery.
From here to there/by Margery Cuyler; illustrated by Yu Cha Pak
Summary: Maria introduces herself as a member of a specific family and as having a
 definite address and place in the universe.
[1. Self-acceptance—Fiction. 2. Mexican-Americans—Fiction. 3. Geography—Fiction.]
I. Pak, Yu Cha, ill. II. Title.
PZ7.C997Fu 1999 [E]—dc21 98-19647

ISBN 0-8050-3191-X / First Edition—1999
Typography by Martha Rago
The artist used watercolor and pastels on Fabriano paper to create the illustrations for this book.
Printed in the United States of America on acid-free paper. ∞
10 9 8 7 6 5 4 3 2 1

*For Jan, who takes me
from Here to There*
—M. C.

To Michael Cho
—Y. C. P.

My name is Maria Mendoza.

I live with my father,

my mother, my baby brother, Tony,

and my older sister, Angelica,

at number 43 Juniper Street—

in the town of Splendora,

in the county of Liberty,

in the state of Texas,

in the country of the United States,

on the continent of North America,

in the Western Hemisphere,

on the planet Earth, .

in the solar system,

in the Milky Way galaxy,

in the universe and beyond.

From here to there, my name is Maria Mendoza.